STONE
EMBRACE

DANIELLE MONSCH

Romantic Geek Publishing

STONE EMBRACE (A STONE
GUARDIAN AFTER-SCENE,
ENTWINED REALMS)
Copyright © 2014 Danielle Monsch
E-book ISBN 978-1-938593-11-6
Print ISBN 978-1-938593-21-5

Publication Date: June 2014

Cover Design: Kix by Design

Interior format by The Killion Group
http://thekilliongroupinc.com

DEDICATION

To the Troublemakers – Cory, Angela, Brandi, and Sarah. Glad you corrupted me.

And, as always, Mr. Jim Garner.

TABLE OF CONTENTS

Books by Danielle Monsch
Chapter One
Chapter Two
Chapter Three
Chapter Four
Chapter Five
About the Author

AUTHOR'S NOTE

Peoples!

Thanks for picking up this short story, but before you begin reading I feel the need to give a heads-up.

This story is not meant to be a stand-alone story. If anything, it would best be described as an extended epilogue to my novel **Stone Guardian** (perhaps eventually I shall add it to that novel and release it as **Stone Guardian: The Director's Cut**... but I digress.)

I have received many amazing and wonderful reviews for **Stone Guardian** (and thank you to everyone who has taken the time to write me or leave a review in a public place). But a common thread developed, where many people expressed some disappointment in both the fact that they didn't see a meeting between Terak and Jack Miller, and also, they wished there was just a bit more hotness in the book. One day on Goodreads, a discussion popped up amongst myself and a few readers of **Stone Guardian** where they reiterated they really wanted more Terak/Larissa lovin'. Being the good author that I am – and being as persuasive as they were – I was ultimately convinced I needed to write this extended after-scene.

Can you read this without reading **Stone Guardian**? Well, sexy times are sexy times, and who doesn't understand a tense dinner with the in-laws? But you will probably be best served by knowing the world and the relationships first.

Enjoy!

BOOKS BY DANIELLE MONSCH

Entwined Realms
Modern-Day Fantasy, where Sword &
Sorcery and Romance Meet
There are no Dragons...are there?

Stone Guardian – *From the Shadows
He Watches Over Her*
Stone Embrace – *In the New Realms,
Love can be the Most Dangerous Battle of
All...*

Fairy Tales & Ever Afters
Slightly Twisted and Very Sassy takes on
Fairy Tales

Loving a Fairy Godmother – *Don't
Fairy Godmothers deserve a little lovin'
too?*

Loving an Ugly Beast – *Can't an Ugly Beast get a little lovin' here?*
Loving a Prince Charming – *When you are Prince Charming, everyone wants a little lovin' from you.*

Pleasure Chronicles

Sexy Sci-Fi about Warrior Women and the Alpha Males who love them

Pleasure Satellite – *To the Strongest goes Everything...*

And want to know whenever a New Book is Released?
DANIELLE MONSCH ANNOUNCEMENT LIST!
http://www.daniellemonsch.com/dani/sign up/

CHAPTER ONE

Now was the answer. The question? *If there was* one *time you wished you were an unashamed alcoholic, when would you choose?* Forget the knife, the tension here could hide a pack of werewolves amidst its layers.

They were at the dinner table, Terak at one end and her father at the other, with her and Michael on either side of Terak and the other three brothers in the middle. Michael didn't look happy, but unlike the rest of the Miller clan, he had no obvious issues with Terak being there.

Terak was in his human form. After an aborted first attempt at meeting her family – where Jack Miller made damn sure to let her know she wasn't off the hook for bringing over her mate and in the same breath made damn sure she knew he wasn't happy about it – Terak refused with the full-force of that gargoyle stubbornness to meet her family in anything but his shifted state, saying he would give her family time to know him. The problem with that – *THE problem? Try problem number seven-hundred and twenty-three* – was illuminated the moment Jack Miller's eyes took in the tall human next to her. Confusion ruled her father's face for a long moment when he saw the man beside her, but the detective's mind pieced together recalled information at lightning pace, and when Jack got *it* – that everything she told him was true, gargoyles could shift into humans, and so many things Jack had believed since the Great Collision had been a lie – suppressed and impotent fury wrote itself deep into the lines of a face that never once showed those emotions in this home.

Larissa's tongue was numb from all the times she had bitten it tonight, and she reached for a glass of water more to feel the cool liquid slide over the abused flesh than because of thirst. Under the table she stroked Terak's hand, the fist the only outward sign of the gargoyle's own distress.

In their bedroom earlier, it had been he who insisted they come today. "They will never accept me if they don't come to know me, *Meyja*. You expect too much, too soon."

She sat on the bed with her back against the headboard and legs stretched before her. Her gargoyle was putting a shirt over his now-human chest, the sight as impressive as always, and an irrational wave of anger overlaid her already rational anger at her father. Because her gargoyle was trying to cater to her father and gain favor, she was going to be denied the sight of that chest all evening. Stupid parental figure. "I *expect* my father to respect the male I have chosen to join my life with. I expect him to not act like a *jackass*."

Fully clothed, Terak came to sit beside her legs and took her hand in his clawless one. "He will. That he did not betray my secret – betray my Clan – to the human authorities tells me he will. But you are asking him to go against the core of his beliefs in taking me as a mate. It is unfair to ask him to make that transition in an instant without giving him time and space to adjust and to grieve."

"Grieve?"

"Yes, grieve," Terak affirmed. "Grief over what he feels is a betrayal of his oath as the leader of the police. And this also lays bare once again his grief over the loss of your mother."

Terak's now grey eyes were direct on her, no hint of shading to tell her he was minimizing his own concerns to make her feel better. Her chest hurt, unable to contain the swell of adoration this male evoked in her, the pure gratitude that she had been blessed enough to have him come into her life. She stroked down the sharp plane of his cheekbone. "There's a very small, vindictive part of me that wants to tell him he can't use her as an excuse for his actions forever. But I never will, because the instant after that impulse occurs, I imagine my life if something were to happen to you, and I know for him it's not an excuse. And afterwards, I want to hug him in apology, because I'm in awe he survived as well as he has."

Strong arms pulled her against a hard chest, and thank gods in this form that smell of newly-cracked stone and undefinable male remained, the smell that was only and forever Terak. She held tight, dragging his warmth and strength into her, both for tonight and for banishing that momentary terror the thought of losing him always evoked.

Of course, now facing her father in the dining room of her old home as he was blatant in his disregard of Terak, the earlier council of giving her father time and space was heading into the territory of *don't think so* and a down-and-dirty yelling match became more inevitable by the minute. "Dad," she said, trying once again to engage Jack in a way that didn't involve him staring a hole through Terak, "How are things at the precinct?"

"I'd rather not talk about it." *In front of him* rang through Jack's tone and down the center of the dining table.

That was it. Larissa near sprang from her seat as she locked gazes with her dad. "Can I see you in the study for a moment?" Damn straight her teeth were clenched – so were her hands, her stomach, all the way down to her toes. No more of this.

Jack rose, defiance in the slow, steady movement. "Yes. Let's go." And he walked ahead without waiting for her to come beside him, like he usually did.

She brushed off Terak's hand and went after her father. The door click was still echoing in the room as she said, "*What* is your problem? We talked about this already."

"We didn't talk," her father shot back, restrained fury in his tone. "You waltzed in and informed me you were marrying a creature. Wait, that's not it, you *mated* a creature. You left not five minutes later while I was still stunned. How is that talking?"

A tiny tremble of guilt fluttered through her stomach, but she wasn't going to let that derail her from setting Dad straight. "It doesn't matter what word is used. He and I are together forever and are *it* for each other. Words are meaningless."

"I am your father, and you can be damn sure it isn't meaningless to me if my daughter is married or not!" Jack paced around the desk, hands on his hips and fire in his eyes. "You didn't talk through *anything* with me. You leave me in the dark while you are in danger. You trust strangers over family. And when it's all over, you leave it to Michael to tell me everything – you can't even face me and explain what was going through your head!"

"I'm twenty-six years old! I don't owe you explanations, Dad!"

"Is that right, baby girl?

Deep breath...deep, deep breath. Her father had a point, and yeah, he was owed an apology for that. "I handled things poorly, and I'm sorry about that. But Dad, if anyone can understand the kind of confusion having your life upended like that can cause, it's you. People and creatures coming at you, and this terror of something so much bigger than you, and you can't tell friend from enemy. The aftermath of all that was chaos, and somehow in all that Michael got hold of me and told me about the panic over me and Taneasha, but I couldn't get away so I had to trust him to handle it." Larissa paused, bringing breath deep into her lungs to calm the panic even the memory of that time could instill in her. "I am sorry. It wasn't how I wanted to let you know. At the time it seemed the only way and looking back, I still don't know how else I could have done it. But I waited until I could tell you about Terak myself. I never wanted you to think I was ashamed of him, because I never will be."

"Then why did you come in here and tell me and then run?"

"Because I don't know what the hell I'm doing?" She threw her hands up in the air, needing physical movement to dissipate the tension building. "You think I don't know how it looks to you, or that I *like* you're not happy about who I love? Of course I want your approval. Never thought it was a possibility I'd ever be without it."

They were toe-to-toe, prize fighters eyeing each other from their corners, each breathing a little hard as if they had gone a round. Long, still seconds, and then Jack broke off the stare, plunking down into the leather chair behind the desk, a long, low exhale accompanying the movement.

Larissa pushed her hair behind her ear, watching as her father let his head fall back against the top of the seat. His age was showing, lines and grey hair somehow more pronounced than they were even a few weeks ago.

How would Laura Miller look now, if that hellish moment never happened? How much grey would streak her hair? How deep would the lines around her eyes be? Would her mom feel differently about Terak, defending her daughter's choice to her stubborn husband? Maybe it was self-interest talking, but something deep inside Larissa warmed, and there was no doubt in what her mother would say. Laura Miller knew all about love – great, deep, abiding love. She experienced it with this stubborn, ornery man sitting behind a desk. Laura Miller would tell her without reservation to stand beside Terak.

Larissa stood before her dad and held nothing back. "I know how I feel. What I feel is eternal, and it's only him. Part of the reason I love him is *because* he is a gargoyle, and that honor and nobility he possesses because of it, the way he'll stand between me and anything that would come after me. I find him beautiful, no matter what. But that doesn't mean I know how to explain *this*. This love, this attraction, how I went from being a sheltered girl and a low-level teacher to being the mate of the Clan Leader of the Gargoyles, responsible now for this Clan that isn't even my same species. It's too big sometimes for me to think about. I realize you have doubts, Dad, and I understand why, because looking at it from the outside, it's impossible."

Jack hunched forward, his elbows resting on his thighs while his hands hung loose between his knees. Whole conversations took place behind his eyes, his mouth tight while the debate as to what he should say played in his head. "I don't doubt you when you say you love him. I see it, Larissa. And if I was young and idealistic, I would send you off with blessings and pretend that was all that was necessary. But you have to know somewhere inside you, this situation is wrong." He leaned up then, a fierce resolve playing over his features. "You cannot stay with him. It's only going to end up bad for you. And if that truth isn't enough to make you walk away, then the fact it will end up bad for him should."

"Dad, we discussed-"

"You discussed like two people in love discuss, which means jack shit." His words cut across hers like a sharp blade. He stood then, facing her fully. "Do his people really want you there? Don't bother to answer, because we both know they don't. They wouldn't want you there, as the *mate* of their leader, even if you had grown up with them. You think they're thrilled a human is wandering their compound and in charge of them?"

No, they weren't. Malek, a few others were openly supportive and true friends and allies. The majority were reserved with her, still judging and waiting. Then the final portion, a vocal minority, and their contempt could be felt through the grey walls of the keep.

It wasn't the easiest situation, but being with Terak was worth it. If he was worth dying for, he was worth fighting for.

And she had already proved he was worth dying for.

"It doesn't matter what they think. They asked for Terak to be their leader knowing I was part of the deal. They may not be joyous over me, but they'll accept me."

"You think so? You are a *risk* to them. With this weird power you have, you'll never be safe from the necro-" Jack's voice faltered, stuttered over the word that was the greatest threat to her safety. For one moment his eyes grew round and haunted, the knowledge of what the death of a beloved truly meant stark in those eyes, before he cleared his throat and continued. "You will always be targeted, and you will always represent a risk to their safety. If things heat up like this Fallon woman claims they will, what do you think the gargoyles will do in order to protect their Clan? What do you think they'll do to Terak if he tries to stop them?"

Goosebumps. One tiny portion of the goosebumps dotting her skin and the shivers descending over her body could be attributed to worry over herself. But Terak...was her father right? Would they force her removal, and what would they do to Terak in order to accomplish that? "They wouldn't have invited us back..."

Jack's hard voice cut through her weak protest. "They probably hoped he was going through a phase, an obsession with something foreign to them, and that he would grow tired of you and set you aside once he came to his senses."

"He won't."

"Maybe he will and maybe he won't, but do you really believe they are not going to force his hand? I raised you smarter than that."

And as she opened her mouth the door swung open, and Terak stood in the doorway.

CHAPTER TWO

With almost forty years on the force
under his belt, Jack Miller could claim —
without pride, without ego — that he
knew how to read people. What he saw of
the male before him almost had him
taking a step back before he remembered
himself.

Terak's human face was almost
pleasant as he looked at Larissa. She
walked to him, and with a light, steady
hand he cupped her face, brushing some
hair behind her ear. "I'm fine," she said,
answering an unspoken question.

"I think it is time your father and I
converse. Please, let me be alone with
him. Please," he added again, when
Larissa's usual stubborn nature reared
its head and it looked like she was going

to argue with him. And then his gaze left Larissa's face and came to rest upon Jack.

The quiet menace in that gaze was real. This was not some act put on by a stupid little shit who would piss himself if he ever saw real action. This was a warrior's gaze and a warrior's resolve.

That was fine with Jack. He was ready to have it out.

Larissa left without looking back, and a pang spread through his chest. His little girl didn't even check with him. For her, all she needed was the words of this male to make her decision.

The unexpected loss put Jack on the attack. "I'm assuming you heard most everything. Tell me I'm wrong. Tell me some bullshit how it's going to be fine and your people won't revolt and betray her the first moment danger comes around them."

Jack himself paced with strong emotion, a habit Michael had picked up from him. In contrast, Terak grew still, though the look in his eyes was anything but calm. "You speak of things you know not."

"I may not know everything about gargoyles, but I notice you're not denying my statement," Jack shot back. "It might be called human nature, but its primal nature. It's the core of us that's going to survive no matter what. Her existence threatens your people. Do you think they'll allow that? A woman from a race they consider inferior, who had the gall to marry their leader so he isn't married to a gargoyle girl like he should be?"

"I am not so weak I cannot keep my people in check." Now Terak advanced, his fingers curling inward. What would that sight look like if Terak was in his gargoyle form, where instead of nails there would be claws? "I am very aware of *every* danger to Larissa. I have already taken the needed steps to care for her."

Jack scoffed, holding his ground. "Against your own people?"

Terak stood before him, his stone-grey eyes hard and flinty. "Against *any* enemy. A strike against her is a strike to me, and do I seem one who will not defend myself? You are her father, so I will make myself clear. Any who seek her harm I will kill. I will rip into them with claw and teeth and separate skin from bone from heart. An enemy, a friend, from within either of our Clans – it does not matter."

For the first time in eons, a shiver ran down Jack's spine as he took in the male before him. The will behind those words was absolute, the venom and the truth unassailable. "And if you are gone?" Jack forced the words through a closed throat, and swallowed to loosen the muscles.

Terak backed away, his voice quieted, but that venomous truth in no way diminished. "I have already made my deal with your devil to protect her no matter the circumstances. She is mine, Jack Miller. I fought against feeling for her, but my heart will have none but her. So I will claim her, and I will protect her, and any who become her enemy? I will destroy."

Shards of a long-ago conversation flittered through Jack's mind...

"She made her choice. If Laura Campbell had told me to go away and not bother her, that's what I would have done. It wouldn't have changed the fact I'd love her forever, but I'd never take what wasn't freely given. But she chose me, and eighteen is legal. So I'm going to

marry her and keep her with me, and old man, if you can't accept that, don't expect us to come into your home ever again."

...and he took in the male before him with new eyes. There was nothing to like here. Even if he believed those two loved each other – and dammit, he did, he really did – that didn't change the fact this was a bad match. Larissa was in danger by being with Terak, and as much as Larissa pushed to the side any objections to Terak being a gargoyle, that was no small difference.

But before him Jack saw the same look he was sure was on his face when he confronted Bill Campbell about marrying Laura – flinty determination and the willingness to set the world afire if that was what it took to accomplish his objective.

Bill Campbell was probably chortling in heaven even now, looking at his son-in-law being put through the same hell he'd given as a young man.

After long moments, Jack spoke. "I can't give you my blessing. There's too much wrong here for me to do that. But I can't change your mind and I can't change hers, and I *can't* lose my daughter. So I will say I'll try to understand and keep my fears to myself." And here Jack put the full force of his will in his gaze, on this one point he would not back down on. "But in return you agree to keep me in the loop. You agree I'm going to know if anything is a threat to her, and you'll let me and my boys protect her when we can. Do we understand one another?"

Terak nodded. "We understand one another."

"Good." Something inside Jack relaxed then, something that had been twisted tight since the day Larissa had gone missing from school. With that release it was time to lay some ground rules for his son-in-law. Bill Campbell would approve. "But here's one last thing to understand. You may be some fearsome creature, but I'm her daddy. You hurt her, there aren't enough stone walls to keep me away from you and prevent me from mounting your head on a pike. You think you're a mean sonovabitch? Next to a father who's listening to his little girl cry, you're nothing more than pottery."

CHAPTER THREE

A peculiar energy emanated from Terak, a vibration that had Larissa on edge, had done so ever since he emerged with her father from the study.

The night hadn't lasted long after that, a perfunctory finishing of the meal and giving the expected thanks and parting words. But even as they left her childhood home and arrived back to their Clan and their bedchamber, the weird mood Terak was in didn't abate.

It wasn't safe – *he* wasn't safe – but even as her mind acknowledged, her body remained calm. If there was one truth to her world, it was she never had anything to fear from Terak.

However, it did prevent her from asking what she wanted most to know, about what their talk covered, about where *all* their relationships stood right now.

The tense lines of his now gargoyle form were as bad as when they were fighting for their lives. As wound up as he was, she doubted he'd be going to bed for a long while. "Are you going to go out on patrol?"

His eyes met hers in the mirror. "No. I would not be effective."

That was obvious, not that she'd tell him that. "Do you wish to talk about it?"

"Did he convince you?"

And this promised to not be good. Silly her, thinking maybe the actual dinner itself would be the worst part of the night. "What do you mean?"

"Your father," and the word *father* in that tone was a blasphemy. "Did he change your mind about your place here?"

"My father didn't change my mind about anything. I am where I want to be."

"Are you sure?" No physical change took place, but somehow she could swear Terak wound tighter and tighter, drawing himself in as he unleashed what he had held back earlier. "He did not tell you how you were in danger here? About how you did not belong amongst the Clan? About how *gargoyles* will betray you the moment first possible?"

"He doesn't understand, and you yourself told me to be patient with him. He'll get to know you and he won't have such prejudiced views."

Terak went on as if she hadn't interrupted. "And did he not tell you about how you being here was to invite my death and put me in danger."

Here she paused, the echo of her father's warning rampant in her head no matter how hard she pushed down. The momentary silence was a mistake, as Terak honed in on the stutter. He turned away, the muscles so tight she could almost believe a hard poke would shatter them. "Terak, whatever Dad said tonight, no matter what he brought up-"

"So you believe his words?"

"It doesn't matter-"

"Do you?"

"I'm not saying I believe them, but he might have brought up a good point."

"What point?"

"Terak, quit *this*. We'll talk tomorrow, after you've calmed down."

He came before her, his eyes hot and unwavering. "What point?"

"That I'm a danger to you." And tears fell, as they'd been wanting to since her father thrust the thought at her. "That you're in danger because of me. That they're going to come after me again. Maybe they can't do the spell they wanted me for back then, but what I can do is so rare, they have to come after me again. That I'm selfish to be here with you."

She met his gaze, thick lashes surrounding her stunning eyes, that cornflower blue which would now and forever be the color he associated only with her. In those eyes was a violent swirl of pain, and fear, but what loomed largest when she looked at him was love. Always love. She spoke again, and her words rocked against him with their unexpected force. "I would have died with you."

Ripping pain punched through his chest at the return of those memories, those moments when she had looked at him with such calm intent as the mountain began to crash around them. He cradled her face in his hands. "Never again, little human," he said, his voice roughened. "You must live. That is my one truth in this world. You must live, even should all others die."

She shook her head, an instant negation of his words. "But I can't live without you. I don't want to. And I'm terrified to think I might end up being the cause of your death."

With cat-quick feet, rage began to overtake pain. She could not...*she could not*... "What are you suggesting? That you leave? *Me?*"

His hands prevented her from turning her head, so she settled for closing her eyes, the circles beneath them a blue-black smudge against her pale skin. "I'm not saying that – don't put words in my mouth. But it still hurts, that my selfishness endangers you. I love you so much, I can't bear-"

"No!" How could this evening have gone so horribly wrong? His woman, his *mate*, thinking of leaving him? Never.

Never.

She had taken him into her heart and her body, had pushed past all barriers and filled the empty places within him with laughter and warmth, and now she talked of taking that away? For what? Pathetic fear? Fear for *him*? No, she should fear for any enemy who would dare approach her, fear the pain and death he would bring to them.

He was gargoyle. Skin and marrow and bone he offered for protection, a path awash with the red tide of enemy's blood.

Instinct, ancient and demanding, hot and molten, flared within him.

He was gargoyle. Tonight, his mate would learn *exactly* what that meant.

CHAPTER FOUR

Before her, Terak's wings flared as they did in battle, and the sense of danger she'd been experiencing all night increased a hundredfold. "Terak?"

"You think me so weak I cannot protect my mate?" His voice was a low wash of sound, a growl which caused enemies to tremble in fear.

She was trembling. But fear? No. No, it was something else in her responding to the vibrations of his tone, a deep feminine instinct to this side of him – a side she had often seen in battle, but never here in their bedchamber.

He loomed over her, huge and hard, a male in his prime, a leader who bowed to no one. A warrior god, and she stood before him a sacrifice.

How had she ever forgotten how overwhelming he was? Those hands, strong enough to crush her, stroked the length of her throat in slow, deliberate movement, the light press of calloused fingertips scraping against her flesh accelerating her heartbeat.

He stepped closer, engulfing her, surrounding her, and now his claws, light and sure, running over the thin fabric of her shirt – over her arms, down her back, the slow strokes prickling the skin underneath which strained towards his touch. "This is mine," he said, his voice low and rough. "I will lay low any who seek to separate me from you."

"Terak?" Was that her voice, so high and unsure?

"Take these off," and dark warning threaded itself through his words. "Or have them ripped off."

His face was inches above her, the hard glint in his eyes assuring her nothing he said tonight was for effect. Without conscious thought trembling fingers came to the buttons on her shirt, and one by one she undid the fastenings, all the while his eyes followed the movement with fearsome intensity.

The shirt skimmed her arms and fell from her body, and now her bra...and here she paused to take in the pure possession in his face, which only grew as his gaze rested on the slope of her breast, still covered in sky-blue satin.

His arms shot out, gathering her wrists above her head in one hand, and his mouth descended over her nipple. The rough wetness of his tongue could be felt through the thin material, and Larissa groaned, head falling back and eyes shutting against his ministrations.

His mouth was firm and warm and wet, giving her small, firm nips through the material between the long, firm stroke of his tongue.

Marking me. He's marking me.

This was so unlike him. He was always gentle with her, touching her as if she were fragile glass. *Gentle* was not the word she would use now.

Rip of fabric, and cool air hit her wet nipples. Now his mouth covered her, the nip from his teeth sharper, the pull in her belly deeper now that there were no barriers, only his mouth on her.

First on her breasts, then he lifted his head so his mouth covered hers, a controlled plundering where he dominated, forcing her mouth wide, the smallest scrape of fang eliciting a gasp and a swirl of heat through her belly.

Her wrists were released, and claws traveled down her back, dragged her jeans down the length of her legs in an explosive burst of movement, leaving her in front of him in only her underwear.

Without warning he turned her, moving her at his pleasure. She leaned against him, her back to his chest. His mouth was hot where neck met shoulder while the tips of his claws played with her nipples, the tiny nip of pain tightening them to pointed tips. His tail curled around her calf, warm and strong and supple, massaging the sensitized length of her leg.

"Are you mine, *Meyja*?" His voice was urgent, rough. "Will you leave me?"

Reason prodded against the murky swirl caused by the myriad of sensation in her body. *That's* what this was about? He was scared she might leave? "Never, I swear. Terak, I'm yours."

One hand left her breast to run across her stomach, never going low enough for her. She canted her hips upwards, but he remained in control, not allowing her any relief. She tried to rub back against him, but he held her away, his hold firm.

His tail moved up her leg, moving against her in sinuous rhythm, urging her legs apart, a demand she eagerly complied with, and she sobbed in relief as finally, *finally,* he rubbed against the edge of her clit.

Wave after wave of sensation crashed through her. Terak brought his wings in front of them and surrounded her, enveloped her. Her senses were filled with him, the sharp point of his teeth against the back of her neck while his hands continued to play with her breasts, pinching just to the point of pain, before rubbing over the hard nub in pure sensuous caress, and during all this his tail firm and strong against her, making her tense in near release and then it would still, slow, let the mounting sensation abate and leave her to cry out in frustration.

"Are you mine?" came the dark velvet whisper in her ear.

"Yes." Her answer was a sob, a supplication. Anything to have him *finish.*

One final hard press of his tail, and then the wings opened and the tail withdrew, and he bent her over the bed and thrust into her. It might be the position, or it might be he was so overpowering, using her as he wished, but he felt huge inside her, almost uncomfortable as her body adjusted to him.

There was no gentleness. His hand against her shoulder blades bent her deeper into the bed, tilted her hips higher, and his body owned hers with each forceful motion of his hips.

The clamp of his teeth on the nape of her neck pushed her over into orgasm, her body shaking so hard Terak faltered for a moment before he resumed his motions, hard and firm and fast, working her body for every last shudder of pleasure.

Even as her body came down from the high, Terak still moved, still pushed into her with his full strength. There was no respite. Her body barely had the final tremor of pleasure when he pulled out and flipped her onto her back, gathering her legs over his shoulders and sliding into her again.

He bent low over her, his mouth capturing hers again. Her nerve-endings were so sensitized it was too much – his mouth, the heat of him, the thrust of his body, the scrape and slide of skin against hers. Her mind was pure white, any rational thought quieted. All that remained was primal longing. Her mate fucking her, using her, forcing her to submit, burying himself in her and marking her with sweat and come.

He pulled up and took her legs from over his shoulders and pushed her knees to her chest before parting them. She followed his gaze and gasped to see herself so open, see in full measure his cock sliding in her, disappear into her and his pelvis crushed against hers for a moment before he slid out, his skin slick and wet and shining from her. He groaned above, and as if her gaze spurred him on his hips moved even faster, and he asked "Are you going to come again, mate? Do you wish me to let you come again?"

Where had this dominating male been hiding inside her gentle gargoyle? He owned her, and with every word he showed he reveled in it. She raised her arms, curled her nails in the hard mass of his biceps. She licked her lips, and would have smiled at the answering groan if she wasn't panting. "Yes, mate. Let me come."

"If I do, will you take my cock in that hot little mouth and swallow me down?"

Oh *fuck*. It was too much, and once again her orgasm surprised her, shook through her body and tightened every muscle as if an electric current was flowing through her.

He slowed, kept working her through every aftershock, as her body bowed and shuddered under him. He moved until she let out one last low groan and relaxed.

Only then did he withdraw, letting her legs fall back on the bed. Only then did he gather his cock in his hand and moved up her body, moving to her side and presenting it in front of her mouth.

She took it eagerly as she lay there, swallowing it down in one long stroke. The taste was pure eroticism, her taste strong at first but then the smell and sensation that was pure Terak coming through.

In this she answered the question he had been asking her all night, by her total submission to him and his needs. Her tongue stroked over the hard flesh while her throat massaged him in the deepest way possible.

His groans grew louder with every moment, and it wouldn't be long before he would come. She worked harder, wanting him to come so she could swallow.

His hands wandered over her face, worked through her hair, his fingers flexing to grab hold of the curls. He grabbed tight and guided her movements, held her close while he pushed his cock down her throat. The movements were slow and deliberate, controlled enough so no harm came to her, but insistent, dominating. His voice was dark and rough, velvet scraping over rubble. *"My mate. My love. Mine."* And then his growls, the most erotic sound in the Realms, as his back bowed and his wings flared, and she drank him down, greedy, hungry, wanting every part of him.

When she gazed upwards, it was to the site of his head thrown back, his chest rising and falling in deep movement. As if sensing her eyes, his gaze came down to meet hers, but it was not completion in his face. Instead, it was sharper, fiercer, the hunger in him not yet satisfied. He glanced down her body and his lip curled, a snarl emitting from his throat.

She followed his gaze, and a heat that came from embarrassment crept through her body. Her legs were sprawled open in wanton invitation, the curls between her legs noticeably damp. Before she could close them his hand was there, his fingers invading her, pushing inside her receptive body.

"Terak," she said, voice a small plea.

In swift movement, he gathered her two hands in his one and pressed them above her head. The continued domination had the same effect as it had all night, making her grow wetter around his thick fingers. "No, little human. For all of tonight, you are mine."

CHAPTER FIVE

She woke to Terak's claws raking through her hair and her body deliciously sore, well-used in the best sense.

His strokes were gentle and bordering on hesitant. So her gargoyle was back to himself, having left the demons which drove him last night to the darkness. She shifted so she was lying on her back, looking up towards Terak.

His eyes were hooded, and he wore no smile on his face. And when he voiced a somber, "Larissa," she knew what was going on in his head – and she was going to put a stop to it.

"You didn't hurt me. Everything we did last night was something I wanted."

"I was too rough—"

"Did I say no? Did I say stop? Go away? I don't want this?" With every question she awaited his acknowledgement, waited for him to shake his head, and after he had done so, she continued, "If there is one thing I know, I know you would tear off your wings with your own hands before you would ever harm me. You are my *mate*, Terak. You are my love and my beloved. And you are a gargoyle. So if that means things get a little..." and here Larissa faltered, images and sensations pressing against her, cutting off the righteous indignation and reminding her how wanton and carnal she behaved last night. Heat traveled over her body, a mingling of renewed desire and embarrassment.

Strange, but it was this reaction that seemed to finally relax Terak, more so than her verbal defense. His body lost the taut gravity, replaced with smug satisfaction. "So my mate enjoyed what I did to her last night?"

"Don't get cocky," she shot back, not giving him the satisfaction of looking away, no matter the burn in her cheeks meant there was a good chance she looked like she had a sunburn. "I'm not here to stroke your ego."

He bent down and brushed his lips over hers. "No," his voice a deep, wicked whisper. "You stroked other things, did you not?"

Last night he was in charge, but now she was back in the game. "I think it was you who was doing the stroking. All I had to do was open my legs, and there you were, every part of you, rubbing over me to make me wet and make me beg." She leaned up, giving his earlobe a gentle bite before whispering, "I was begging my mate to let me come. I begged him to make me feel like only he can. You're so big all over, and only you can fill me. You like filling me, don't you? You like pushing into me when I'm wet and dripping for you?"

"*Yesss.*" It was almost painful, how he sounded now, and unlike last night, he was at her mercy. Time to flip him over and ride him like a bucking bronco.

Which is what she did. She barely had to push before he was on his back, and their mingled groans when she lifted her hips and joined with him told how ready they both were for this.

Last night was dominance, was pushing fear away with physical mastery. Now was recommitment, as his hands on her hips steadied and lifted her, as her hands on his chest moved in caressing strokes across his skin while she accepted and loved him in the most primal way a female could with a male.

Larissa took him deep, relishing each slide of flesh and the groans that came from deep inside him, telling of how much of a hold she had over him. Her gaze locked with his, and she willed him to see everything – love and devotion and that she would never *falter*, would never, to the end of her days, leave his side. He was hers, and she was his, and nothing would change that.

His breathing became ragged and her body responded, everything in her tightening to match his quickening rhythm. He pushed her back against him faster, harder, and her nails scored his chest as her body was abused in the most pleasurable way imaginable.

Terak surged upwards into her, once, twice, and a loud, long growl erupted as he emptied himself into her, her muscles tightening around him as she found her own release, her cries lost in his.

Collapsing against him, Larissa drifted, only peripherally aware of the cooling sweat on her skin and her labored breaths in the still morning air.

"What you do to me, little human." The voice was rough, though the humor was unmistakable.

"And I plan to keep doing it to you for a very long time, because I'm not going anywhere, and neither are you." Larissa pushed up, looking down at her lover's face. "I'm scared, Terak. I'm not ashamed to admit that. We're in the midst of something big. I hate that you're in danger – I'm allowed to hate that, I'm allowed to hate I'm a danger to you – but I can't leave you. So I listen to my warrior mate when he tells me how to stay safe, and I take every precaution to make sure I never do something stupid that puts you at risk."

The look in his eyes – adoration, gratitude, devotion – kept her enthralled. "I will gladly take every danger known to keep you at my side. Never leave me, Larissa. Not even to protect me."

Her beautiful gargoyle. She leaned down, bestowing on him the most gentle, most loving kiss she could, willing every emotion she felt for her protector to be expressed through breath, lips, skin. "You by my side, and I'm at yours, and we'll never leave, no matter what else happens in this world. Right?"

His fangs brushed against her lips, his claws raked down her back, and his tail wound around both their ankles, binding the two of them together. *"Right..."*

The End

NOTE FROM DANIELLE MONSCH

Peoples! Thanks for reading **Stone Embrace**, a short story in the *Entwined Realms* world. Please leave a review – reviews help authors so *so* much, and we are so grateful for them! ☺

If you'd like to read the book that started it all and have not already, I direct you to **Stone Guardian (Entwined Realms, Book 1)**

And if you are interested in hearing about my other books and want to know as soon as they are released, please sign up for my newsletter! Newsletters are sent out only when a book is released or I'm giving stuff away, and your email is never used for any other purpose or sold/distributed to anyone else!

http://www.daniellemonsch.com/dani /signup/

STONE GUARDIAN

Entwined Realms, Book One

Gryphons flying past skyscrapers? Wizards battling it out in coffeehouses? Women riding motorcycles with large swords strapped to their backs? All normal sights since the Great Collision happened twenty-six years ago.

Well, not normal for everyone. Larissa Miller may have been born after the Great Collision, but as a history teacher who lives in the human-only city, she has never come into contact with any other race or species, nor has she wanted to. Her life is as ordinary as it gets - that is, until one day she walks out of her apartment and is attacked by a mob of Zombies, only to be saved by a Gargoyle.

Gargoyles trust no one outside their Clan, but due to a cryptic prophecy,

Terak, Leader of the Gargoyles, has been watching over the human woman for months. While he can find no reason why the woman has been singled out, something about her stirs every protective instinct within him. When the attack confirms that the threats against her exist and are real, he convinces Larissa that though their races have never been allies, the best chance of discovering why she has been brought into his world is by working together.

In the course of their investigation Terak becomes entranced by his little human. But when he discovers why Necromancers want her and the great reward that awaits him if he betrays her, he must choose between the welfare of his Clan and not only Larissa's life, but the fate of this New Realm as well.

Buy **Stone Guardian** now!

ABOUT THE AUTHOR

Born to the pothole-ridden streets of Pittsburgh, PA, Danielle Monsch started writing in a time long ago, a time when there were not enough vampire stories to read and she had to write her own to fill the void. Yes, such a time of darkness did indeed exist.

Danielle writes stories full of fantastical goodness and plenty of action, but always with lots of romance (and a bit of woo-hoo!) mixed in. Vampires and Werewolves and Demons and Angels, Sword & Sorcery, Fairy Tales, Updated Mythologies and the like – if it's out of the ordinary, it's fair game for her stories.

Go to:

www.daniellemonsch.com/dani/
for one-stop shopping with everything to do with Danielle - there you can join her newsletter (*highly* encouraged as it contains all info about upcoming books, plus lots of random surprises) follow her on twitter, and like her on facebook. Just want to send Danielle a quick email? Easy enough, that's Dani@DanielleMonsch.com.